Lulubell
Ladybug

Mrs. Ladybug was having a bad day!

It was washing day, and she
had so much to do.

The baby ladybugs needed feeding, clothes needed mending and the beds needed making too!

"Don't worry, Mommy,"
said little Lulubell.
"Now I'm a big ladybug,
I can help. I'll go and get all
the things you need – then
you will have less to do!"

"Oh, that would be so helpful, Lulubell,"
said Mrs. Ladybug.
So off Lulubell flew.

The first person
she met was
Miss Spider.
"Hmm, you look tasty!"
cooed Miss Spider.

"Please don't eat me," pleaded Lulubell.
"I need some thread. If you can spare me
some of yours, you can…"
and she whispered in Miss Spider's ear.

"That would be nice," agreed Miss Spider.

When she got to the pond,
she met Mr. Frog.
"Mmm, you look tasty!"
croaked Mr. Frog,
licking his lips.

"Please don't eat me," said Lulubell.
"I need some water, and if you give me
some of yours, you can..." and
she whispered in Mr. Frog's ear.

"Yes please," nodded Mr. Frog.

Lulubell bumped into Kitten
playing in the garden.
"Ooh, you look tasty!"
purred Kitten.

"Please don't eat me,"
squeaked Lulubell.
"I need some toys, and if you can give
me one of yours, you can...."
and she whispered in Kitten's ear.

"Lovely!" meowed Kitten.

Then Lulubell met Early Bird,
who was looking for worms.
"You look tasty!"
twittered
Early Bird.

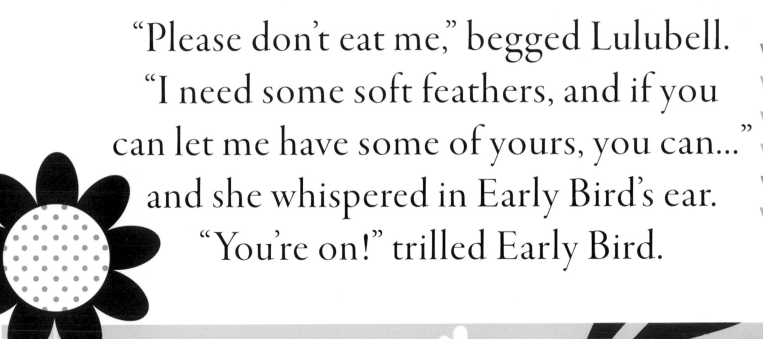

"Please don't eat me," begged Lulubell.
"I need some soft feathers, and if you
can let me have some of yours, you can..."
and she whispered in Early Bird's ear.
"You're on!" trilled Early Bird.

"Phew!"
breathed the worm.

Lulubell met Mr. Squirrel,
who was collecting nuts.
"You look tasty!"
chattered Mr. Squirrel.

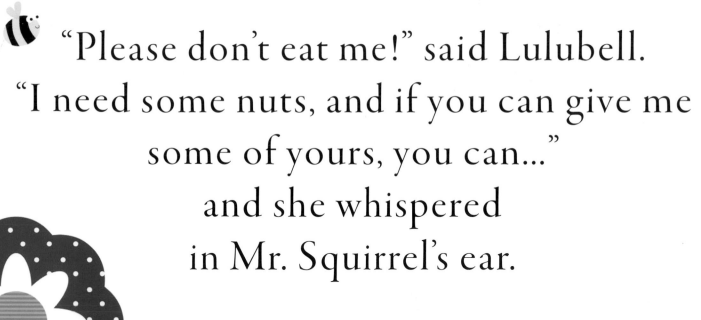

"Please don't eat me!" said Lulubell.
"I need some nuts, and if you can give me
some of yours, you can..."
and she whispered
in Mr. Squirrel's ear.

"Perfect!"
cheered Mr. Squirrel.

Pleased with her day's work, Lulubell fluttered home.

Her tired mom was pleased to see her back,
safe and sound.

"Well done, Lulubell!"
said Mrs. Ladybug.
"You have saved me so much work.
What a caring little ladybug you are!"

"No problem!" said Lulubell. "Everyone was kind and generous."

"I just had to promise one tiny little thing."

"I promised they could all come for tea!"

For: Maisey

First published in 2016 by Rockpool Children's Books Ltd.

This edition published in 2017 by Rockpool Children's Books Ltd.
in association with Albury Books.
Albury Court, Albury, Thame
OX9 2LP, United Kingdom

Text and Illustrations copyright © Sam Walshaw 2016

Sam Walshaw has asserted the moral rights
to be identified as the author and illustrator of this book.
© Rockpool Children's Books Ltd. 2016

Printed in China

ISBN978-1-906081-83-6 (Paperback)

"How nice," sighed a weary Mrs. Ladybug. "You really are a caring little Lulubell!"